N nut

O owl

P present

Q queen

R rug

S spider

T turtle

U umbrella

V vase

W walrus

X xiphias

xylophone

Y yarn

Z zipper

moth

moose

mouse

mushroom

moss

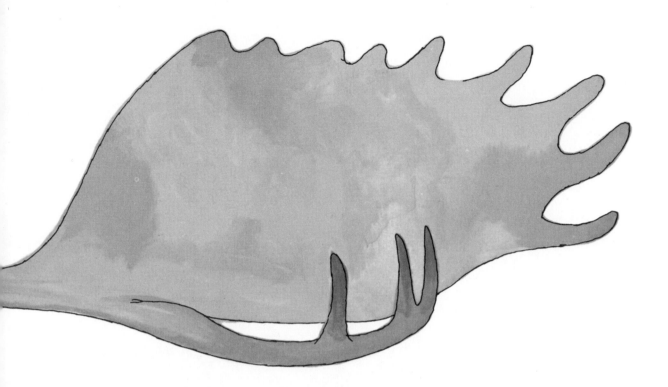

# Richard Scarry's
# BEST WORD BOOK EVER

mosquito

A GOLDEN BOOK • NEW YORK

curtains

sun

window

# THE NEW DAY

It is the morning of a new day.
The sun is shining.
Kenny Bear gets up out of bed.

washcloth

soap

toothbrush

toothpaste

towel

First he washes his
face and hands.

Then he brushes
his teeth.

mirror

comb

pajamas

He combs his hair.

shirt

pants

He dresses himself.

He makes his bed.

He goes to the kitchen
to eat his breakfast.

Kenny Bear sits in
his favorite chair.

He is very hungry.
This is what he eats—

cold fruit juice

warm cereal

with cream

pancakes

with butter and maple syrup

He doesn't eat
the toaster.

fried eggs

bacon

toast

muffins

honey

jam

hot cocoa

cool milk

and a waffle.

When he finishes eating breakfast he helps
wash and dry the dishes.

cup          saucer          plate          bowl          fork     knife     spoon          glass

jar          pitcher          frying pan          pot     lid     pan          bottle     juice squeezer          glass

Now he is ready to play with his friends.          7

# THE RABBIT FAMILY'S HOUSE

Father Rabbit, Mother Rabbit, and the
Rabbit children are getting ready for
the new day. Their friend Owl
is waiting for the children
to come outside.
Can you find him?

chimney

roof

mirror

lamp

bed

Big
Brother's
bedroom

cupboard

dining
room

kitchen

sink

Father

table

back door

chair

floor

axe

stove

Mother

woodpile

lawn

birdbath

WHOO

owl

smoke

antenna

light switch

television set

record player

hassock

Mickey

bunk bed

bathroom

upstairs hall

Molly

bedroom

front door

living room

candle

outside light

picture

telephone

fireplace

stairs

sofa or couch

front hall

doormat

rug

window

stone walk

9

# PAINTING AND DRAWING WITH COLORS

Painting and drawing are fun.
You can use bright colors.
You can paint with brushes
or even your fingers. You can
draw with crayons or pencils.
What do you like to draw?

finger painting

paper

make orange

make green

pencil

eraser

pencil drawing

make violet

make pink

make gray

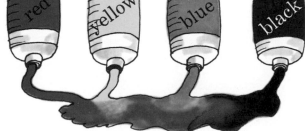
make brown

water dish

smock

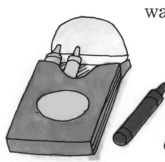
poster paint

watercolors

paintbrushes

crayons

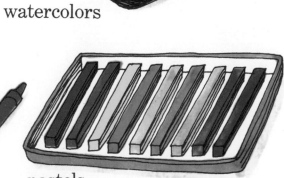
pastels

10

# TOYS

Sometimes it is fun to play by yourself. Sometimes it is fun to play with your friends. What are your favorite toys? Do you like to play with blocks?

rocking horse

tricycle

electric trains

truck and loader

blocks

scooter

glider

robot

building set

croquet

# AT THE PLAYGROUND

The children are all having fun doing different things. Which children are doing the things you like best?

seesaw

slide

leapfrog

hide-and-seek

somersault

ring-around-a-rosie

jump rope

ladder

rings

swing

sliding pole

top

roller skates

bubble blowing

kite

jungle gym

merry-go-round

tag

hoop rolling

ring toss

jacks

marbles

sandbox

kite string

bouncing ball

hopscotch

13

# TOOLS

hammer

nail

Everyone is very busy
working with tools.
What tools do you have
in your house? What
would you like to build?

pushpin

axe

ladder

log

carpenter

board

saw

sawdust

sandpaper

hacksaw

vise

drill

plane

woodpecker

jigsaw

wood shavings

screwdriver

screws

pliers

file

14

bucksaw

trowel

bricklayer

hoe

brick wall

cement

brick

lumber

fence painter

paintbrush

ball of twine

sawhorse

paint

barrel

tack

tack hammer

hatchet

ruler

folding ruler

jackknife

toolbox

square

putty knife

shovel

bolt

nut

dirt

monkey wrench

compass

wheelbarrow

pickaxe

glue

15

silo

weather vane

crow

scarecrow

disc harrow

field

tractor

barn

hayloft

goat

stall

milk can

tin can

pail

farm truck

wagon

hen

rooster

baby chick

pigsty

Kathy Bear is going
to feed the pig.

corncrib

16

haystack

cow

apple tree

farmhouse

water pump

meadow

fence

sheep

horse

clothesline

apple

grass

clothes basket

# THE BEARS' FARM

Kenny Bear is going
to feed the chickens.

The Bears are working hard on their farm.
What are they all doing? What is the duck doing?
What is the scarecrow supposed to be doing?
He is not doing it, is he?

chicken coop

mailbox

well

duck pond

duck     ducklings

bee

pitchfork

beehive     17

weather instruments

blimp

microphone

control tower

# AT THE AIRPORT

The air traffic controller is talking to the pilot of the jet passenger plane. The controller is giving the pilot take-off instructions.

baggage train

waiting room

binoculars

tourist

observation deck

camera

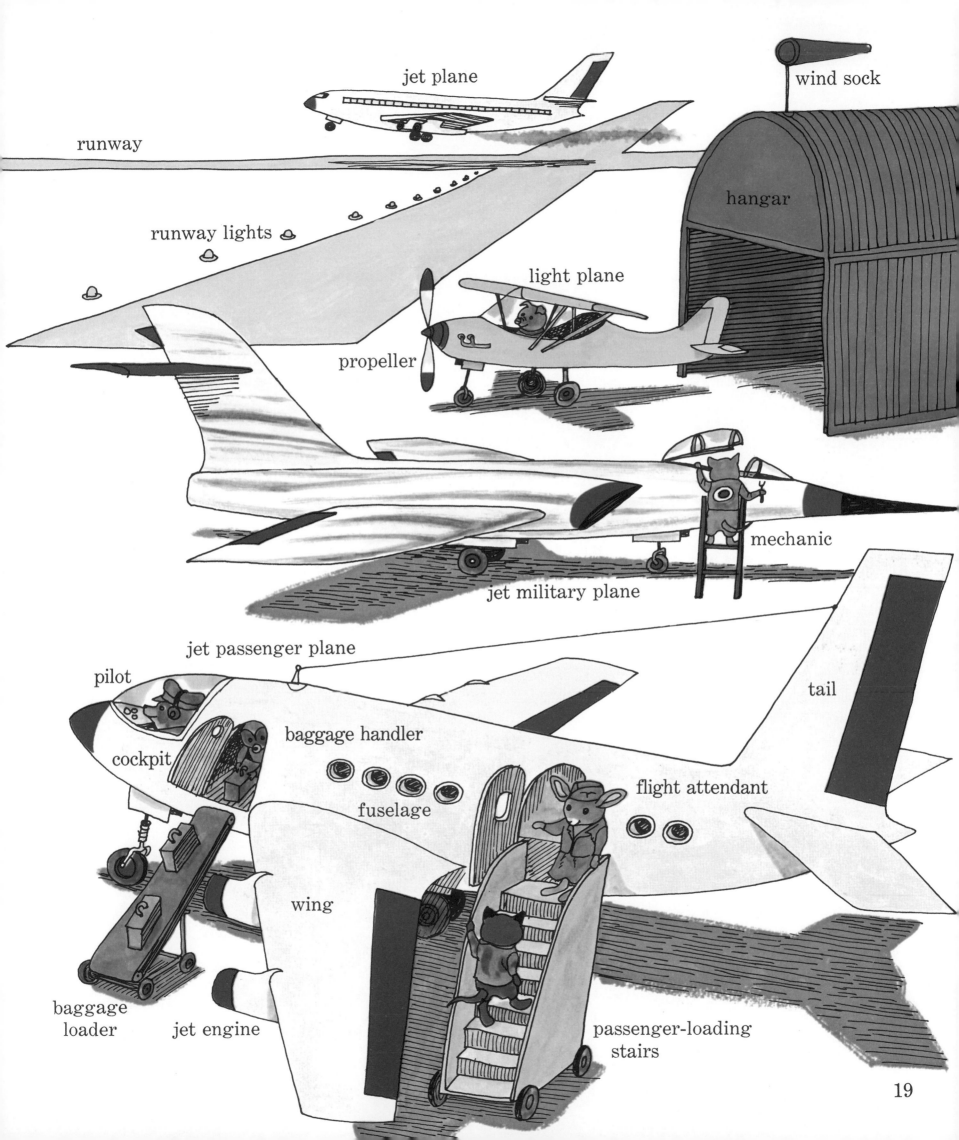

jet plane

wind sock

runway

hangar

runway lights

light plane

propeller

mechanic

jet military plane

jet passenger plane

pilot

tail

cockpit

baggage handler

flight attendant

fuselage

wing

baggage loader

jet engine

passenger-loading stairs

19

meat
cleaver

hook

ham

saw

scales

**MEATS**

wrapping paper

twine

butcher

pickle
barrel

garbage
pail

bologna    frankfurters    hamburger

bacon    chop    fish

steak

a piglet who wants to work
in the supermarket when
she grows up

sawdust

cart

# AT THE SUPERMARKET

The Pigs are buying groceries for their family.
What would you like to buy next time
you go to the market?
Would you like to buy
a pickle?

books

GOLDEN BOOKS

customer

shopper

orange juice

raisins

money

purse

cashier

eggs

milk

butter

ice cream

cash
register

20

FRUITS

pineapple

bananas

scales

grocer

apples

oranges

pears

grapefruit

melons

grapes

lemons

cherries

strawberries

raspberries

blueberries

plums

peaches

watermelon

coconut

pumpkin

cabbage

squash

cauliflower

VEGETABLES

corn

beans

lettuce

tomatoes

asparagus

peas

potatoes

celery

spinach

beets

onions

carrots

cucumbers

turnip

broom

cookies

sugar

cereal

spaghetti

canned food

peanut butter

cheese

salt

apricots

baby food

bread

jam

21

# MEALTIME

The Pig family is having a special holiday meal. There is so much good food to enjoy! What do you see on the table that you like to eat?

carving knife and fork

roast beef

meat platter

tablespoon

coffeepot

teapot

saltshaker

pepper shaker

fork

dinner plate

glass

cream pitcher

knife

spoon

cup

saucer

sugar bowl

napkin

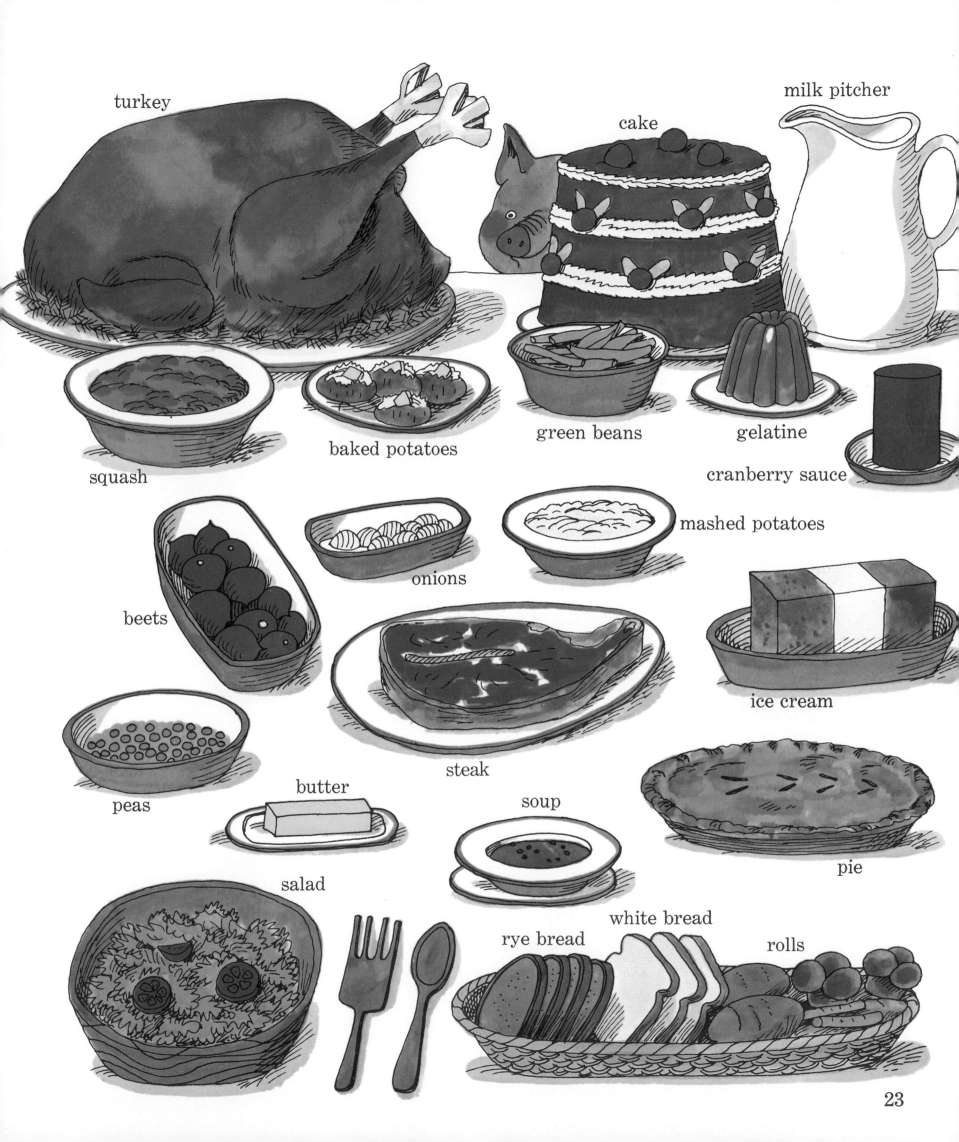

turkey

cake

milk pitcher

green beans

gelatine

cranberry sauce

squash

baked potatoes

mashed potatoes

beets

onions

ice cream

peas

steak

butter

soup

pie

salad

rye bread

white bread

rolls

23

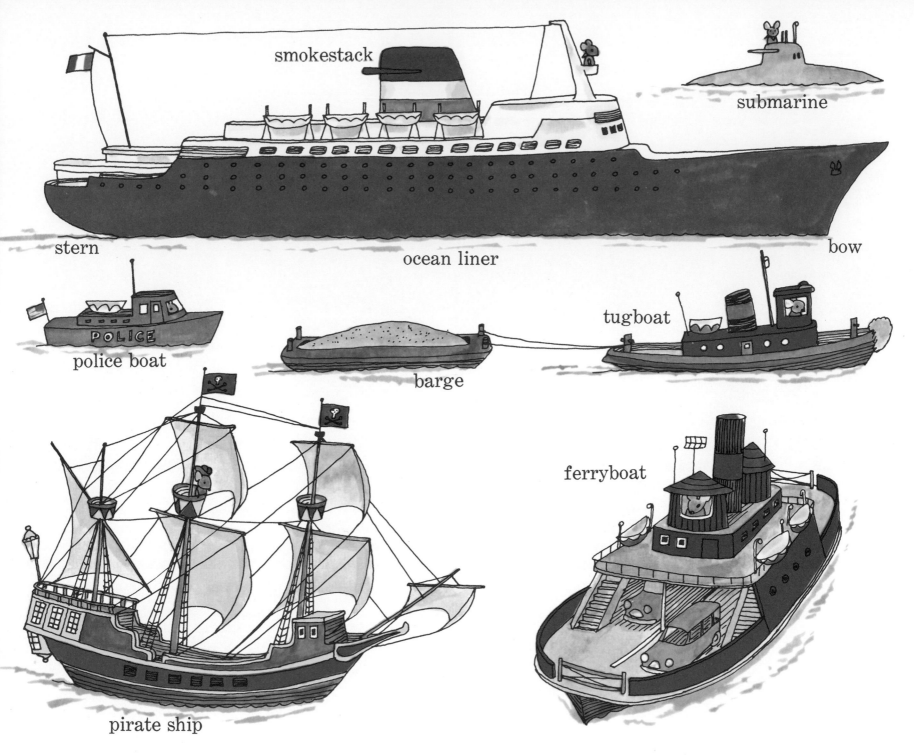

smokestack

submarine

stern

ocean liner

bow

police boat

POLICE

barge

tugboat

ferryboat

pirate ship

# BOATS AND SHIPS

One of the things in the water is not a boat, but it helps boats find the place they want to go. Do you know what it is?

motorboat

paddle

canoe

kayak

oar

rowboat

freighter

lightship

AMBROSE

coast guard ship

CG-7

oil tanker

fireboat

F.D.

fishing nets

fishing trawler

sport-fishing boat

speedboat

10

houseboat

raft

sailboat

THE WHITE SWAN

light buoy

2

25

# KEEPING HEALTHY

Your doctors and your dentist are your good friends. They want you to stay healthy and strong. Will you give your doctors and dentist a big smile the next time you see them? How big a smile can you smile?

gauze bandage

adhesive tape

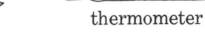
thermometer

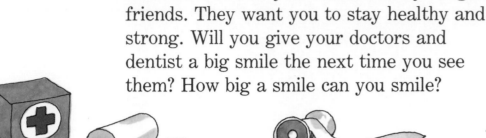
stethoscope

cotton balls

tweezers

plastic bandage
for small cuts
and hurts

scissors

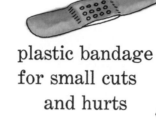
pills

flashlight

eye chart

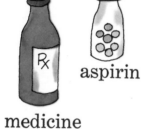
aspirin

medicine

rubber hammer
to make legs kick

tongue depressor
for looking down throats

toothpaste

toothbrush

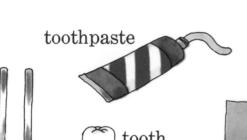

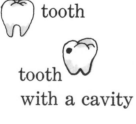
tooth

tooth
with a cavity

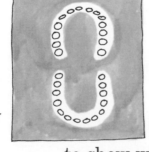
record chart
to show where any
cavities have been found

dental tools

The X-ray machine
can look inside
your tooth to
see if anything
is wrong with it.

The doctor listens to your heart.

scales

hurt tail

doctor

patient

eye doctor

The eye doctor tests your eyes.

dental engine

dentist

rinse bowl

instrument table

water cup

dental unit

dentist's chair

dental hygienist

The dentist looks for cavities and the dental hygienist explains how to care for your teeth.

27

# THE BEAR TWINS GET DRESSED

Kenny Bear awakens one cold, frosty morning. He wants to dress very warmly before going outside.

He yawns and gets up out of bed. He takes off his pajamas, folds them, and puts them in a dresser drawer.

What should he wear today to keep warm?

 pajama top

 pajama bottom

slippers

He puts on his

 T-shirt

 undershorts

 cap

 shirt

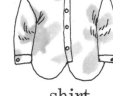 pants

 overalls

 necktie

sweater

 socks

hat

muffler

 sneakers

gloves

jacket

overcoat

raincoat

 and rainhat.

As Kenny is walking out of the front door his father says, "Don't forget to put your boots on!"

 boots

28

Kathy Bear stretches hard before she gets out of bed. She takes off her nightgown and hangs it on the hook in her closet.

What do you think Kathy should wear today to keep warm?

nightgown

She puts on her

underpants

undershirt

hair ribbon

blouse

skirt

sweater

kneesocks

ear muffs

shoes

snowsuit

and mittens.

She puts her change purse

into her backpack.

As Kathy is walking out of the front door her mother says, "Don't forget to put your boots on!"

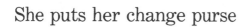

Do you ever forget to put on your boots?

29

deer

lion

elephant

tiger

panda

monkeys

brown bear

gorilla

polar bear

30

buffalo

camel

zebra

zookeeper

giraffe

leopard

sea lion

zoo train

The veterinarian makes sure all the animals are healthy.

# AT THE ZOO

Mr. and Mrs. Mouse took their children to the zoo. How will those children ever be able to get all those balloons into their house tonight? Which is your favorite animal at the zoo?

balloon seller

rhinoceros

hippopotamus

skyscraper

antenna

water tank

church

BOOK PUBLISHER

COSTUMES

NEWSPAPER OFFICE

*Dancing School*

Bookstore

DRUGSTORE

traffic light

apartment house

telephone booth

mailbox

book reader

mail truck

street

# IN THE CITY

letter carrier

Mouse has just bought a book at the bookstore.
She is going to buy a newspaper and then join
her rabbit friends at the sidewalk cafe and drink some
lemonade with them. Show with your finger the way
she will go. Remember to have her look both
ways before she crosses a street.

fire hydrant

32

hotel

street sign

park

park bench

statue

manhole

taxi

RESTAURANT

sidewalk cafe

barbershop

delivery cycle

traffic officer

police car

DANGER

one way

Miss CAT

THEATER

NOW PLAYING

bus

BUS STOP

TAXI STAND

SUBWAY

sidewalk

token seller

subway entrance

newspapers

newsstand

subway station

33

radio tower

ocean

island

# A DRIVE
## IN THE COUNTRY

There are many things to see when you take a drive in the country. Can you see Harry and Sally, the mountain climbers? Can you see what Harry has dropped from his knapsack?

factory

gas station

lake

tunnel

gas pump

tollbooth

turnpike or thruway
or superhighway

farm

bridge

brook

mill

waterfall

stream

picnickers

34

picnic area

lighthouse

beach

crane

fire lookout tower

bay

woods

seaport

drawbridge

hill

tug

mountain

windmill

village

river

pond

log cabin

road

forest

mountain climbers

cliff

knapsack

apple

35

# HOLIDAYS

Holidays are happy times, aren't they?
Which holiday do you like best?
I bet you like them all.

On holidays we visit friends and relatives.
Sometimes we give or get presents.
What would you like to get for your birthday?

horn

New Year's Day

valentine

St. Valentine's Day

Easter

Easter egg

Easter bunny

Easter chick

balloons

rattle

cake          ice cream

Birthday

National Holiday

fireworks

flag

bugle

bass drum

drum

fife

uniform

36

ghost

Halloween

moon

skeleton

witch

black cat

witch's broom

pumpkin

Chanukah

trick-or-treat bag

angel

menorah

candle

Christmas

wreath

Christmas tree

holly

ornaments

tree lights

stockings

beard

fireplace

Santa Claus

bag

present

37

# AT SCHOOL

School is fun. There are so many things we learn to do. Kathy Bear is learning how to find a lost mitten.

pencil sharpener

chalk

chalkboard eraser

notebook

eraser

pencil

fountain pen

ball-point pen

paper

straw

milk

ink

cookies

scissors

string

yarn

paper clip

paste

workbook

storybook

thumbtacks

modelling clay

lost-clothing drawer

38

flag

clock

bell

chalkboard

teacher

calendar

JANUARY

a b c

cat dog

inkwell

map

map stand

wastebasket

artist

pupil

desk

classroom

paper shapes

music teacher

refrigerator

kitchen cabinet

doorknob

can opener

soap

teapot

electrical outlet

counter

freezer

garbage pail

washing machine

dishwasher

Father Pig

laundry basket

eggbeater

eggshell

stool

Annie Pig

measuring cup

mixing bowl

rolling pin

batter spoon

Susan Pig

cookie cutter

dough

Peter Pig

strainer

cookie tray

cake pan

funnel

ketchup bottle

spatula

flour bin

food grinder

sugar bowl

mustard jar

40

# IN THE KITCHEN

closet

feather duster

broom

dustpan

mop

vacuum cleaner

egg timer

shelf

flyswatter

Mother Pig

hood

coffeepot

teakettle

burner

oven

stove

iron

ironing board

All the Pigs like to work in the kitchen. They are making good things to eat. What is Father Pig making? What is Mother Pig putting into the oven?

teaspoon

tablespoon

soup spoon

double boiler

blender

pestle

toaster

mortar

saucepan

corkscrew

ladle

colander

cutting board

measuring spoons

matches

electric mixer

potato masher

saltshaker

pepper grinder

cookbook

carving fork and knife

# WHEN YOU GROW UP

What would you like to be when you are
bigger? Would you like to be a good
cook like your father? Would you like
to be a doctor or a nurse?

What would you like to be?

police officer

fire fighter

sailor

nurse

taxi driver

farmer

gardener

doctor

carpenter

musician

scientist

baker

dentist

secretary

good cook

singer

artist

pilot

fisherman

truck driver

teacher

garage mechanic

reporter

photographer

storekeeper

judge

librarian

dancer

daddy

mommy

# THINGS WE DO

There are many things
that we can do. And there
are some things we cannot do.
What is one thing we can't do?
Look and see.

dig

blow

build

break

sleep

awaken

walk

run

stand

sit

read

watch

draw and write

44

pull

push

kick

talk

listen

shout

whisper

eat

laugh

smile

cry

drink

jump over

crawl under

fall down

we can't fly

peek

tip a hat

go up

go down

go in

come out

# WORK MACHINES

Busy, busy, busy bears. Most of the bears are busy moving dirt with their machines. But there is one bear who has a machine which does something else to the dirt. Which bear is it? What is she doing?

dirt

bulldozer

shovel

dump trailer

tractor scraper

dump truck

tractor shovel

bucket loader

dirt

roller

and tractor

smooth dirt

rough dirt

47

automobile carrier

GASOLINE

gasoline truck

milk truck

broken-down car

tow truck

motorcycle

taxi

sports car

TAXI

48

Golden Wings Freight Line

trailer truck

SANITATION ENGINEER

garbage truck

boat trailer

# CARS AND TRUCKS

Down the street go the
cars and trucks.
But look! Some of the
cars don't have drivers.
Which cars have no drivers?

station wagon

motor scooter

antique car

SCHOOL BUS

school bus

round

square

triangle

diamond

star

crescent

heart

straight

curved

cone

# SHAPES AND SIZES

thin

tall

big

fat

short

little

long

tiny

short

father

mother

# THE BABY

The Cat family has a new baby kitten.
They don't know what to name it.
What would you like
to name the new baby?
Write the kitten's name here.

—— —— —— —— —— ——

uncle

grandmother

bottle

baby

rattle

brother

sister

diaper

aunt

grandfather

playpen

cousin

high chair

stroller

crib

bassinet

play table

walker

baby carriage

# AT THE CIRCUS

The band is playing and the animals are doing their acts. What do you like to watch best at the circus?

tent pole

balancing pole

tightrope performer

tightrope

bareback rider

band

rope ladder

bandstand

circus horse

performing elephant

sawdust

ring

ringmaster

trick dog

clown

pennant

circus tent

trapeze

trapeze artist

acrobat

safety net

ticket seller

hoop

lion

whip

cage

lion tamer

trained sea lion

balloon
seller

juggler

popcorn seller

53

# THE
# FIRE FIGHTERS TO THE RESCUE

Will the brave fire fighters
put out the fire in time?
I think so, don't you?

rescue truck

POLICE

police car

nozzle

rear-wheel steerer

fire engine

hook-and-ladder
truck

hose

ladder

front-wheel
steerer

boots

helmet

first-aid kit

hook

bell

fire alarm box

ambulance

flames

water

smoke

fire chief

cat in
danger

megaphone

fire chief's car

fire fighter

pumper

F.D.
3

fire hydrant

ladder

fire
fighters

rescue net

fire fighter

fire
extinguisher

55

bell

whistle

7

steam locomotive and tender

boxcar

# TRAINS

Which train do you think
would be the most fun to run?
Would it be a freight train
or a passenger train?

lantern

signal tower

handcar

caboose

flatcar

dining car

railroad station

platform

conductor

baggage wagon

56

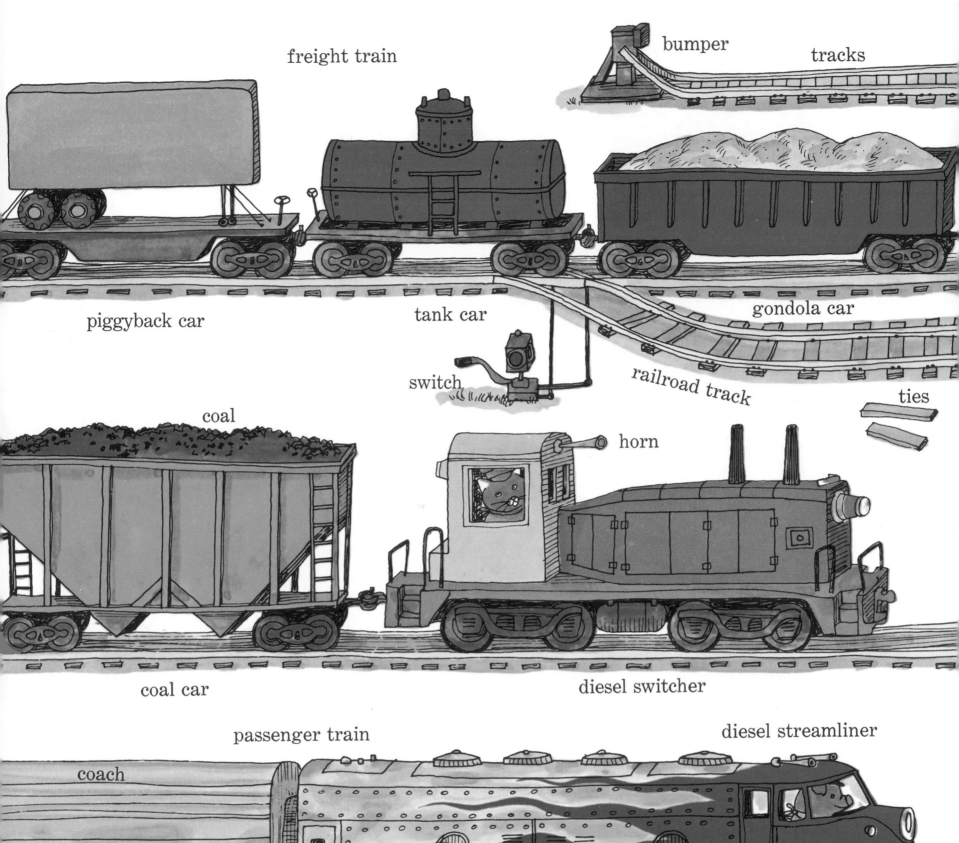

freight train

bumper

tracks

piggyback car

tank car

gondola car

switch

railroad track

ties

coal

horn

coal car

diesel switcher

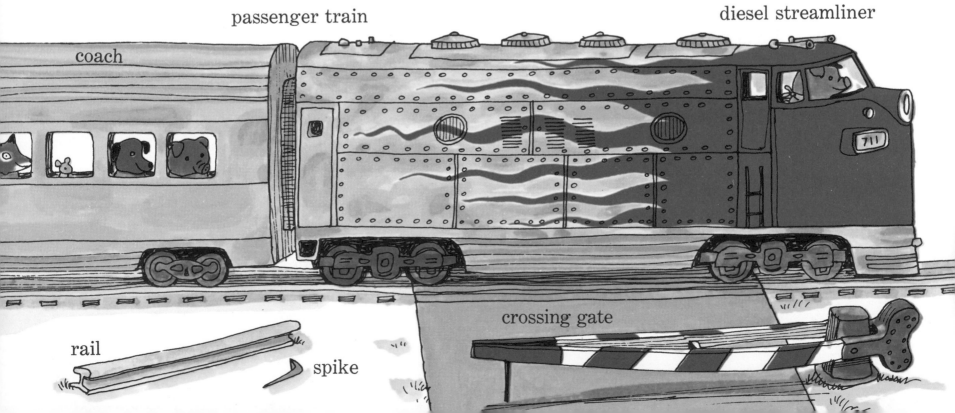

passenger train

diesel streamliner

coach

711

crossing gate

rail

spike

# AT THE BEACH

In the summertime it is fun
to go to the beach.
What do you think
Rabbit hears in the seashell?
Is it the sound of the waves?

telescope

lighthouse

summer cottage

oar

anchor

beach toy

shovel

rowboat

sandpiper

sand castle

waves

skate

bluefish

oyster

lobster

sea purse

hermit crab

clam

scallop

sea gull

umbrella

sun

pavilion

flagpole

sand dune

lifeguard

boardwalk

beach grass

stairs

bathhouse

beach chair

seashell

starfish

sand fort

waves

shrimp

minnow

horseshoe crab

crab

flounder

seaweed

mussel

59

# MAKING THINGS GROW

Everyone is working in the garden.
Mr. Crow has a seed in his mouth.
Do you think he will plant it?
Or will he eat it?

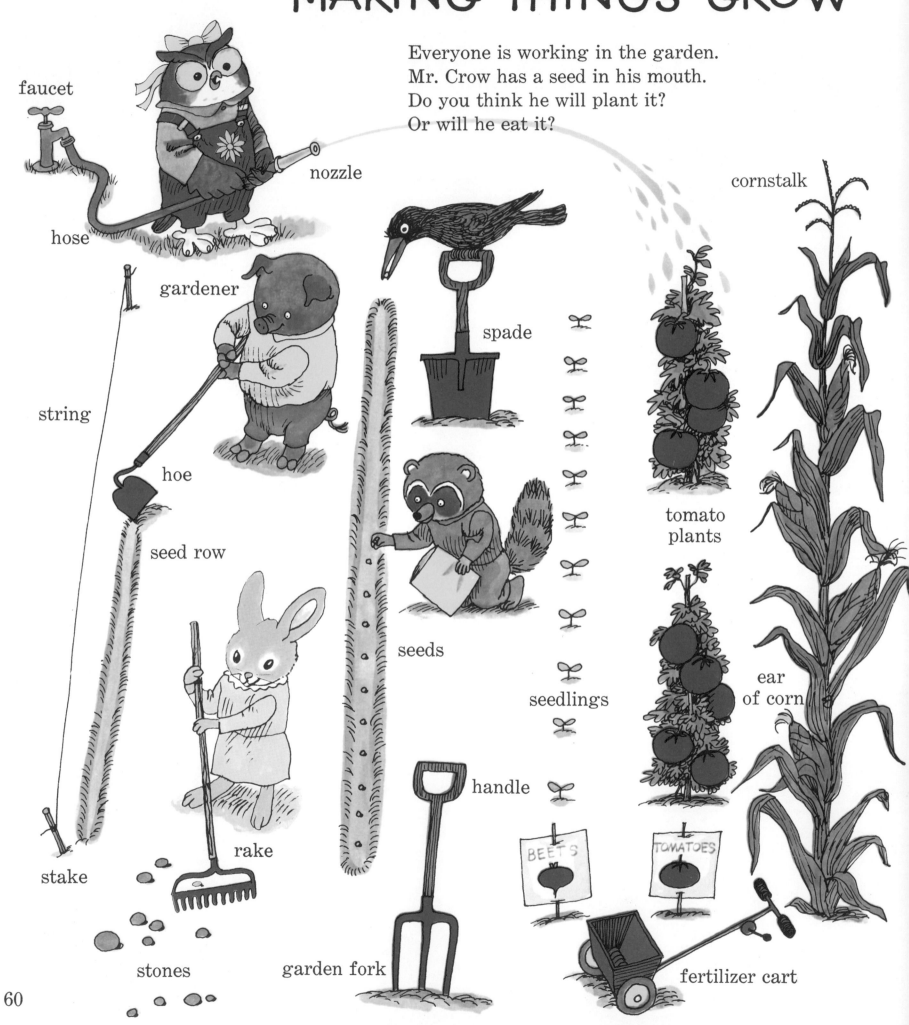

faucet

nozzle

cornstalk

hose

gardener

spade

string

hoe

tomato
plants

seed row

seeds

ear
of corn

stake

seedlings

handle

rake

BEETS

TOMATOES

stones

garden fork

fertilizer cart

# THE WEATHER

sun

cloud

When we go outdoors we see what the weather is like. Sometimes it is sunny. Sometimes it is cloudy. It can be windy, or cold, or hot. It can be snowing or raining. What was the weather like outdoors today? What is your favorite kind of weather?

lightning

rain

hailstones

snowflakes

thermometer

rainbow

windmill

wind

hat

raindrops

foxtail grass

toad

toadstool

ladybug

a cat chasing a hat

puddle

mud

kite

rain shower

plow

robin

buds

nest

# SPRING

Look at that baby lamb hop!
It is spring. She is happy.
Look at Mr. Bear coming out of
his cave! It is spring. He is happy.
Now he can use his new
lawn mower.

tree

lamb

bush

bridge

brook

fern

roots

turtle

cave

spring peeper

pussy willow

daffodil

lawn mower

crocus

violets

62

# SUMMER

cow

meadow

calf

cornfield

fence

Do you like to go
on picnics in the summertime?
Ants just love to go to picnics.
Do you know why?

station wagon

tent

fly

screen

cooking grill

charcoal

picnic basket

cooler

hamburger

ketchup

charcoal bag

hotdog

pickle

mosquito

paper cup

mustard

pole

rock

ants

bobber

cattails

frog

dock

pond

water lily

dragonfly

pebbles

stones

63

sun

duck

falling leaves

corn shock

gate

stone wall

nuts

pumpkin

roadside stand

Indian corn

cider

jelly

squash

# FALL

In the fall the air gets
colder. The green leaves turn to
bright colors. Then they fall to
the ground. Is that why we say
it is fall at this time of year?
Maybe it is.

smoke

flames

basket of apples

turkey

rake

bonfire

64

leaves

snowstorm

# WINTER

There are many ways to
have fun on the snow and ice.
Maybe you would like to do
all of them. Would you?

sleigh

icicle

fishing
shack

skis

sled

ice fishing

toboggan

ice-skating rink

snow

ice skater

snowball

hockey stick

puck

muffler

spare tire

ice skates

jeep

snowman

a pig all wrapped up

snowplow

65

# LITTLE THINGS

Here are many little things.
What little thing do you sometimes
put on your bedroom wall?

worm

dandelion seed

button

spool

thread

fly

ant

drop of water

ladybug

bead

snowflake

pin

fingerprint

petal

mosquito

butterfly

fishhook

crumb

bubble

peanut

tack

pen point

tea leaf

gumdrop

pea

caterpillar

jelly bean

firefly

ring

sand

blueberry

moth

rice

polliwog

keyhole

shell

marble

blade of grass

paper clip

cricket

raisin

beetle

raspberry

thimble

pincushion

hermit crab

pebble

sea horse

bee

mushroom

pearl

ink spot

confetti

feather

splinter

bean

safety pin

dot

baby mouse

66

# PARTS OF THE BODY

Bears use their paws to pick things up.
What do you use?

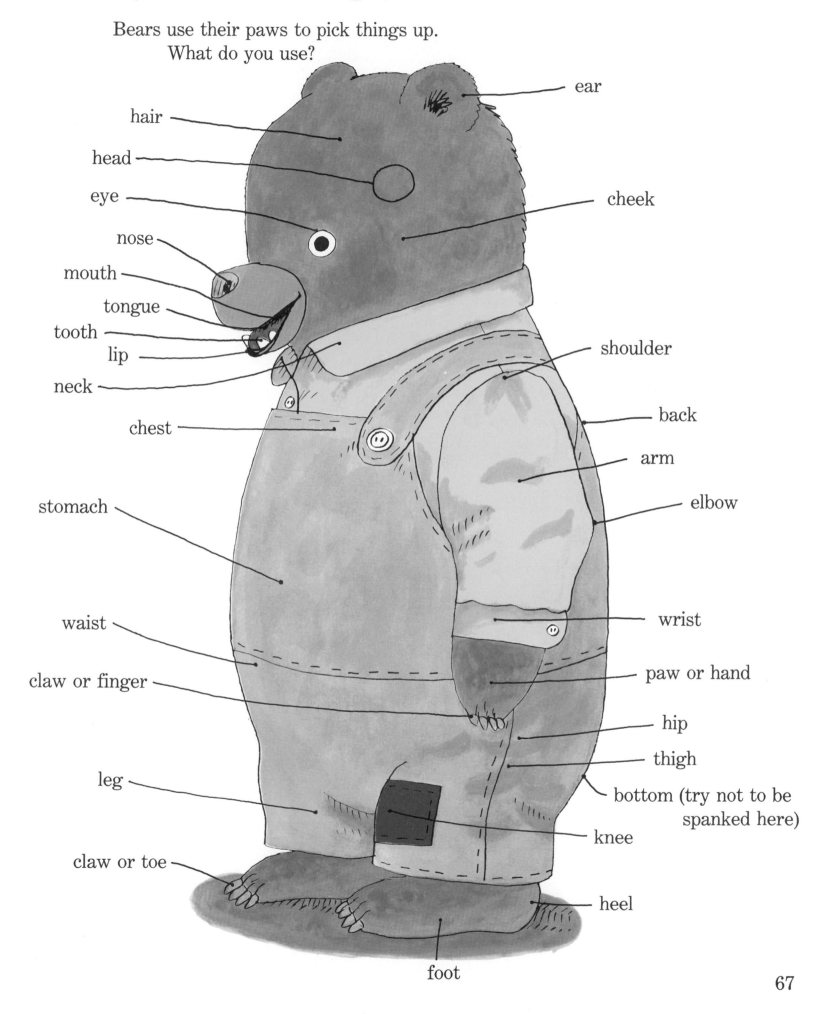

ear

hair

head

eye

cheek

nose

mouth

tongue

tooth

lip

neck

shoulder

back

arm

chest

elbow

stomach

waist

wrist

claw or finger

paw or hand

hip

thigh

bottom (try not to be
spanked here)

leg

knee

claw or toe

heel

foot

# BEDTIME

Little Elephant is getting ready for bed.
But who is that hiding under the bed?
Find that rascal and tell her to brush her
teeth and get ready for bed, too.

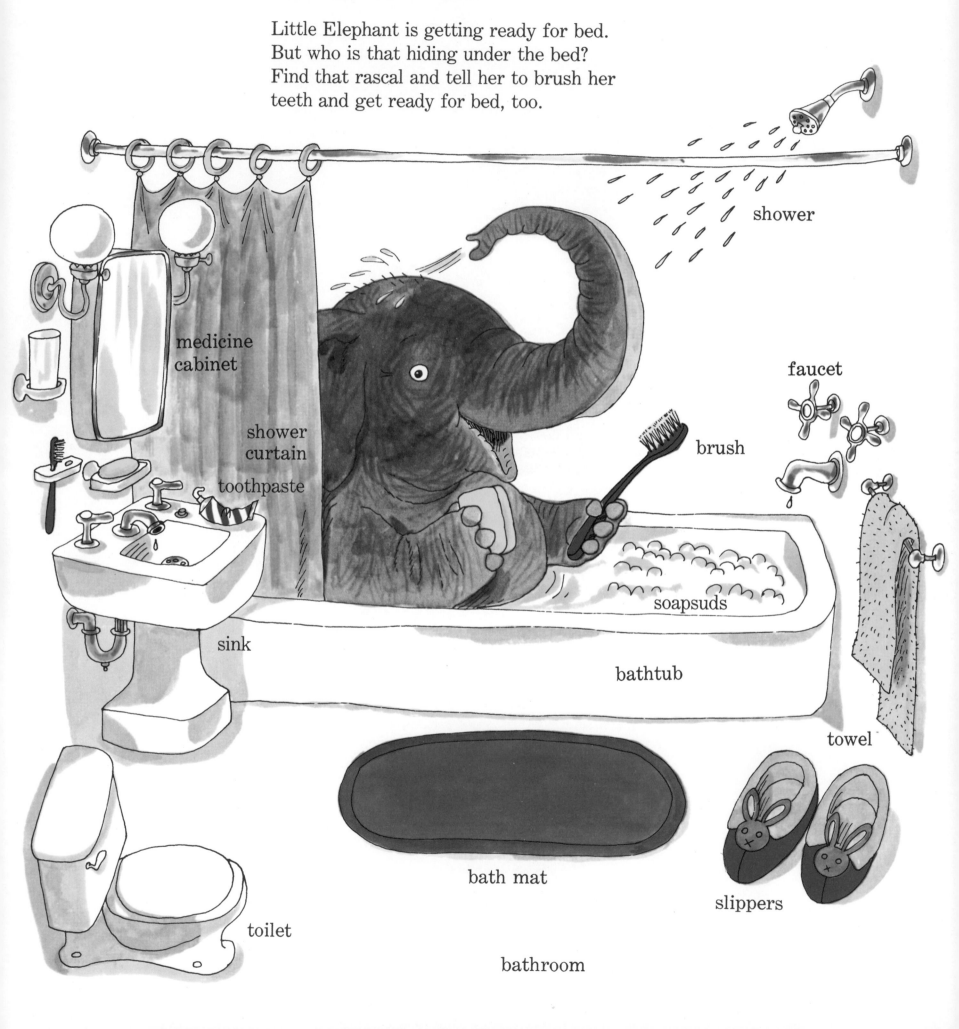

shower

faucet

medicine
cabinet

brush

shower
curtain

toothpaste

soapsuds

sink

bathtub

towel

bath mat

slippers

toilet

bathroom

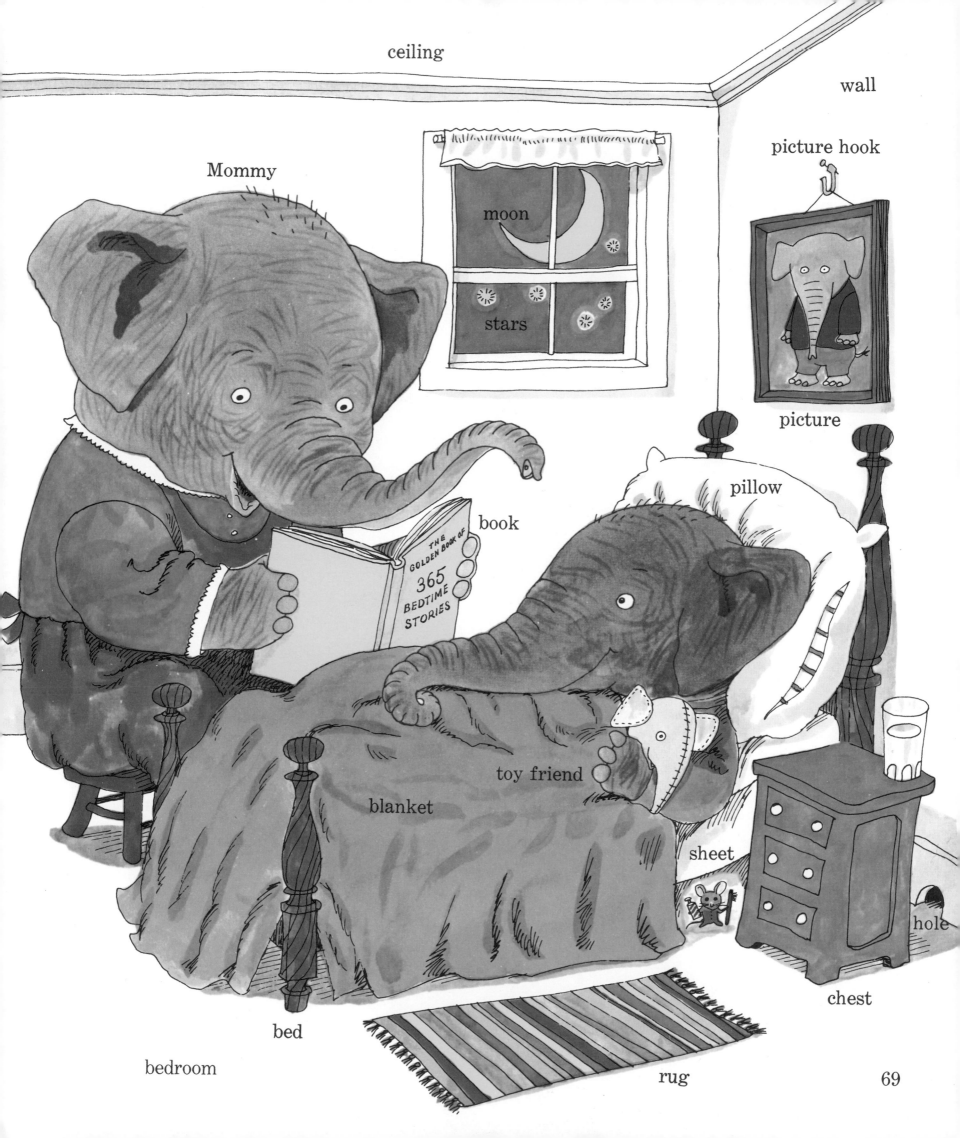

ceiling

wall

picture hook

Mommy

moon

stars

picture

pillow

book

THE
GOLDEN BOOK OF
365
BEDTIME
STORIES

toy friend

sheet

blanket

hole

chest

bed

bedroom

rug

69

# NUMBERS

How high can you count?
Can you count up to
twenty ladybugs?
I'll bet you can.

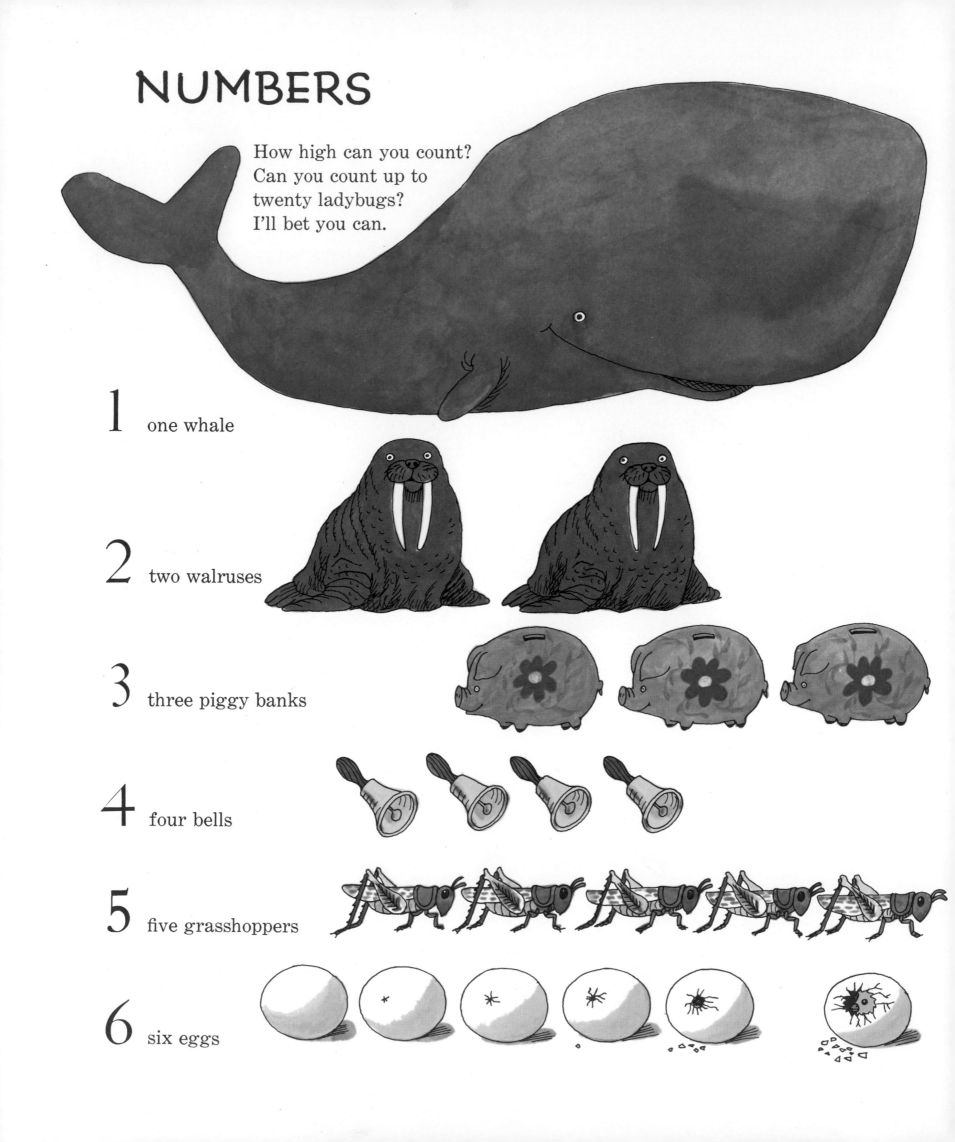

1 one whale

2 two walruses

3 three piggy banks

4 four bells

5 five grasshoppers

6 six eggs